MONSTERS BeGone

written by

Beverly Oliver Carr

This book was born in Beverly Carr's imagination years ago, as she sang it as a song to both of her children, Bobby and Bethany, to scare away monsters at bedtime. When deciding to turn the tune into a children's book, she asked them if they remembered it. Bethany said that she remembered it well! She went on to say when she heard those "bumps in the night" she would sing it to herself for reassurance. "It warms a mom's heart to know that her little girl used her song to help calm her fears during the night."

Other books by Beverly Oliver Carr

"TALES FROM BEHIND THE TEACHER'S DESK"
"LITTLE DEBBIE'S SPECIAL GIFT"

This book is dedicated to
Bobby Carr and Bethany Carr,
the cutest little monsters I ever saw.

To Billy,

I hope you enjoy looking
at all the colorful monsters in
my book and learning the song
in the back.

Love,

Beverly Oliver Carr

There's no such thing as

Monsters!

Red . . .

Green . . .

Yellow . . .

Or White . . .

There's no such thing as monsters,
So you can have a good night!

They can't come in your window . . .

Or climb up through your floor. . .

They can't come through your ceiling . . .

Or come in through your door. . .

There's no such thing as monsters,
Red, green, yellow, or white.

There's no such thing as

Monsters

So you can have a good night!

The End.

There's No Such Thing As Monsters

Beverly Carr

36053337R10017

Made in the USA
Lexington, KY
05 October 2014